VICKY SWANKY IS A BEAUTY

VICKY SWANKY
IS A BEAUTY

DIANE WILLIAMS

McSWEENEY'S BOOKS

SAN FRANCISCO

www.mcsweeneys.net

Copyright © 2012 Diane Williams

This book's cover features a detail of "My Mona Lisa," a 1972 painting by
Croatian artist Ivan Generalic. The image appears with the kind permission of
the artist's family, and is copyright © 2012 the estate of Ivan Generalic.

McSweeney's and colophon are registered trademarks of McSweeney's,
a privately held company with wildly fluctuating resources.

ISBN: 978-1-936365-71-5

CONTENTS

Perfectly safe; go ahead.
　　—DIANE WILLIAMS

MY DEFECTS

I'm happy at least to do without a sexual relation and I have this fabulous reputation and how did I get that in the first place? I am proud enough of this reputation and it stands to reason there's a lot that's secret that I don't tell anyone.

I want to end this at the flabber, although I am flabbergasted.

I opened the cupboard, where the treats are stored, and helped myself and made a big mess, by the lakeshore, of the food, of the rest of my life, eventually.

Michelle, the doctor's nurse, showed me a photograph of her cats. The smart cat opens the cupboard, Michelle says, where the treats are stored, and she can help herself, and she makes a big mess!

I crossed the street to survey the lake and I heard crepitations—three little girls bouncing their ball. I used to see them in perspective—my children—young people, one clearly unsuitable. She can't help herself—she makes a big mess.

With my insight and my skill—what do I search for at the shore?—the repose of the lake. But sadly, although it does have a dreamy look, it is so prone to covering familiar ground.

BETWEEN MIDNIGHT AND 6 AM

Women were not a major ingredient in my thinking at that time.

She was blonde, very small, and if I remember right she had big breasts. Uh, Arthur was sleeping on a couch in the living room so I can imagine there was traipsing going on. Mother had her bedroom next to the kitchen. The girl had to go through the apartment in order to get to the bathroom.

I spent the night on the stairs, not dozing off.

She was a bankrupt.

As for me, I could have put more into this. Mother wants her sons to get ahead.

It must have been very soon after that that Mother said, "*Ohhhh, Ka-a-a-a-a-y!*"

We loved Kay better than we loved our mother. But by glancing back, as I approach middle age, the scale of things quite slowly, calmly, becomes a peep-show.

And everybody had to share. And there was a sliding glass door into the breakfast nook—so there was a curtain over it.

I met with some success. I took a job as a chemical mix-man—to store, order, and prepare wet and dry chemicals.

O Kay!

I'm only warming up. Most of my work is routine labor. There's an element of physical danger. It is not easy to have this job. I'm not the outdoors type.

Today I got the temperature level too high in the chemical levels in the glass plate processing room and had to get buckets of ice.

Sometimes I'm over a barrel—my wife and I agree.

To get anywhere in my life at this time!—rather, to get anywhere near my wife at this time!—that can take days. I have to go through the kitchen, the laundry—I have to go through hell! Not entirely true.

I ate by myself.

I went to our bedroom with a glass of water for her in the hopes of hearing her cheery cry.

She's so warm—she's kind and she'll likely say, "Hi!"

Her hands were folded behind her head. She whispered, modestly.

This will pep me up.

From all outward appearances, there was substantial risk for lack of concentration, overenthusiastic response, unrealistic desires, emotional craving, weak discipline, pettiness, a tendency to show off, and temporary stops to take a breath.

IF TOLD CORRECTLY
IT WILL CENTER ON ME

Jack Lam sat me on the bed. He didn't sit me—first he had to park the car.

Then Jack Lam sat briefly himself, put his chin down, frowned. I acted as if I was biting the top of his head—setting my teeth on, not into him—not to mention the fact that I was also swallowing darker areas.

Over the next seven years that I kept this project close in mind, I came to understand that my devices belonged to a lost age.

I took measures.

Jack had lost his vigor. I was unwell.

My luggage was packed. I'd be solitary when I arrived in Tarrytown. Stella Arpiarian still had The Curio Shop. Nikos had gone back to Greece.

I like Jimmy here. I have to face Marlene.

I heard the dog next door making a good imitation of what my asthma attacks sound like. Everyone is sounding like me!

Don't forget me!

PEDESTAL

He had chafing and I'm not having luck with anything I'm using. We had agreed to meet where they know me. The server put drinks down.

"Hey!" he said. "I happen to have a chicken. Why don't you come over?"

I would say that to a friend, and it would be true!

My anus is now irritated. My vagina's very delicate. My stomach hurts.

His sconces were shaded in a red tartan plaid and there were side-views of sailing boats in frames.

I was getting to see the hair cracks in his skin that suggest stone or concrete as it hardens.

Back out on Ninety-first Street, a man and a woman were walking their dog. The woman had turnip-colored hair. The man wore a felt hat and he motioned to me. They could have both been exhausted and penniless. No! As it turned out they were assembled there to talk me out of that. Let me think about this further. At a stand, I bought a few strands of daisies. Every bone in one of these blossoms is mended.

DEATH BED

"Now, say good-bye to your mother," Ruth Price says, "before you die."

I've got that confident feeling.

Then we hear the toilet bowl water.

"Go away!" I said to Mother.

Everybody in the original cast appears at my door—my father who was the President of the United States; Mother, who was also a President of the United States. I was a President of the United States. My two children are here who have been Presidents of the United States. My neighbor Gary Dossey who was in my high-school graduating class was a President of the United States.

GLEE

We have a drink of coffee and a Danish and it has this, what we call—grandmother cough-up—a bright yellow filling. The project is to resurrect glee. This is the explicit reason I get on a bus and go to an area where I do this and have a black coffee.

I emphasize, I confess, as well, that last night I came into a room, smiled a while and my laughter was like a hand on my own shoulder. As I opened up the volume of the television set, I saw a television beauty and a man wants to marry her and she says, "I don't do that sort of thing."

While in their company, the woman changes her clothing and puts down an article of clothing and folds it. How finely she shows us her efforts. Even as we have that behind us, the man speaks. His side-locks are worn next to his chin and his hair is marred by bright lights. The woman's head is set against a dark-purple shield of drapery. But when something momentous occurs, I am glad to say there is a sense of crisis.

And for Vera and me—we are no exception. I've lived for years. In Chicago our sunsets are red creases and purple bulges and we can amuse ourselves with them.

MY FIRST REAL HOME

In there, there was this man who developed a habit of sharpening knives. You know he had a house and a yard, so he had a lawnmower and several axes and he had a hedge shears and, of course, he had kitchen knives and scissors, and he and his wife lived in comfort.

Within a relatively short time he had spent half of his fortune on sharpening equipment and they were gracing his basement on every available table and bench and he added special stands for the equipment.

He would end up with knives or shears that were so sharp they just had to come near something and it would cut itself.

It's the kind of sharpening that goes beyond comprehension. You just lean the knife against a piece of paper.

Tommy used to use him. Ernie'd do his chain saws.

So, I take my knives under my arm and I drive off to Ernie's and he and I became friends and we'd talk about everything.

"I don't sharpen things right away. You leave it—and see that white box over there?" he'd said. That was his office. It was a little white box attached to the house with a lid you could open and inside there were a couple of ballpoint pens. There was a glass jar with change. There were tags with rubber bands and there was an order form that you filled out in case he wasn't there.

He wasn't there the first time I came back, at least I didn't see him.

I went up to the box and those knives were transformed.

As I was closing the lid, he came up through the basement door that was right there and we started to chat and he has to show me something in the garden, so he takes me to where he has his plantings. It's as if the dirt was all sorted and arranged, and then, when I said he had cut his lawn so nice, he was shining like a plug bayonet.

All the little straws and grass were pointing in one direction.

"I don't mow like my neighbor," he said.

Oh, and then he also had a nice touch—for every packet he had completed there was a Band-Aid included. Just a man after my own heart. He died.

I was sad because whenever I got there I was very happy.

BROOM

I felt, off the start, right at home with him in this gorgeous New England spread-out home with a fantastic lawn and a pond with an island on it where Olivia de Havilland had gotten married and a tennis court and vegetable garden and a rose garden and what time of the year was it? *Hmmm.* Must have been summer because he introduced me to sweet corn and he had Platt, who lived to be twenty-two years of age and who died shortly after I got married—a cat.

He was sitting in front of the fire going through his briefcase that was filled with office business and now and then he'd toss pages and pages into the fire and then he would stop, he'd pet Platt and say—*The poor pussy, such a bad life for a cat!*

One day after he had gone through a large amount of papers to be tossed and when he had chucked them into the fire—there was a lesson for us. We were chased out of the house by a rough sound and we looked up at the chimney and saw a violet broom of fire sticking out of the chimney. It just burned itself out and nothing was hurt, but that's how a lot of his houses burned down.

Some people speak of an energy stream in a village site or sacred place.

I put my arms around him, released him.

Such business as his! A corner of his stair hall was covered by old dry leaves that yield all by themselves.

ON THE JOB

He looked like a man whose leader has failed him time after time, as he asked the seller awkward questions—not hostile. He was looking for a better belt buckle.

The seller said, You ought to buy yourself something beautiful! Why not this?

He paid for the buckle, which he felt was brighter and stronger than he was. His sense of sight and smell were diminishing.

He could only crudely draw something on his life and just fill it in—say a horse.

"Can I see that?" he said, "What is that?"

It was a baby porringer.

At the close of the day, the seller counted her money, went

to the bank—the next step. She hates to push items she doesn't approve of, especially in this small town, five days a week, where everything she says contains the mystery of health and salvation that preserves her customers from hurt or peril.

That much was settled, as the customer entered his home, approached his wife, and considered his chances. Hadn't his wife been daily smacked across the mouth with lipstick and cut above the eyes with mascara?

She had an enormous bosom that anyone could feel leaping forward to afford pleasure. She was gabbing and her husband—the customer—was like a whole horse who'd fallen out of its stall—a horse that could not ever get out of its neck-high stall on its own, but then his front legs—their whole length—went over the top edge of the gate, and the customer made a suitable adjustment to get his equilibrium well outside of the stall.

"It's so cute," he said to his wife, "when you saw me, how excited you got."

His wife liked him so much and she had a sweet face and the customer thought he was being perfectly insincere.

He went on talking—it was a mixed type of thing—he was lonely and he was trying to get his sheer delight out of the way.

MOOD WHICH GRIPPED ME

To a ludicrous degree I could have been in a very good mood looking forward. I am going to be married—followed by dessert, fruit, and bonbons in dishes.

And my furniture cheers me up. We sat in side chairs, packed with springs or foam, accompanied by a moth, who lounged.

It turned out Wayne had been missing me. He was depressed and had, therefore, come to my enclosure after many months.

So Wayne and I now loitered at the edge of the room, ahead of my marriage to Jim.

Over across the—how can I make this wonderful?—the large turf bog!—the sky showed fewer than a hundred birds and at its near top, zero.

Wayne said caringly *—It hurts me that I can't stay because I was unfaithful once or twice.*

Wayne! Stay! Jim said.

I was too restless to save time. I leaned against dear Hallam, and Ardolph—isn't he wise?—a divine spear?—a linden on a hill!—a man from the east who has come to the west. He is well born, noble, a home-loving wolf.

Wayne said, *Lady, you owe me up the wazoo!* He resumed his departure which is such a gloomy tradition.

Another one of my boyfriends said helpfully there is a great difference between love, hatred, and desire, but nothing compels us to maintain these differences.

THE USE OF FETISHES

"I was a lucky person. I was a very successful person," said the woman. She was not entirely busy with her work. She took cups and tumblers from her cupboard to prepare a coffee or a tea. She thought, We have some smaller or even smaller.

Her Uncle Bill said, "Have you been able to have sexual intercourse?"

She said, "Yes! And I had a climax too!"

This idea is compact and stained and strained to the limit.

WOMAN IN ROSE DRESS

Her sex worries will be discussed when people worry what happened to her at the end of her life when her chin droops and when her eyes are hooded. Not yet.

Her fervor and her youth irritate her for they provide a sort of permanent entry into a shop. She lifts a bouquet of broccoli rabe. Oh, how awful it is!

"I don't know how to cook these. Do you cook the leaves?"

The man says, "You chop off the ends and chop them up—look!"

She's got some pent-up gem on her finger. (Those colored stones, they're all cooked, you know.)

Didn't she used to appreciate its rays of light? And she used to appreciate the man.

Ask yourself sincerely at odd moments, "Am I prone to deep feeling?" for it is less than necessary—that very small, bright, enlarging thing. The passions do not knock one out, but they may permit you to have carnal complaints before proceeding further. Let's visit another woman—Deirdre—and then Donna. What's more—Doris grew up exhausted by shock and word of mouth. She hadn't been married long, it was a spring day, and she was uninterested still in her own love story.

WEIGHT, HAIR, LENGTH

They had admired a bronze sphinx with an upraised paw and an elegant and extremely fine clock on skinny legs.

The husband tried to buy a jug, enameled and gilded.

A number of his parts are modern and wide. He looks well made for sustained and undemanding and justified indulgence.

COCKEYED

She was cockeyed on her settee—her face considerably close to the cushioned seat. She righted herself, but she dropped the book.

She was sick and her mother had died of typhoid, her sister of parasitic worms.

This had been one of the few occasions when she had been charming and tactful.

There were bruises on the lady's face and indications of other injuries upon her delicate structure.

Her library table desk is made of sycamore, painted in the classic manner—the type of thing that seems peculiar.

THE WEDDING MASK DOOR PULL

They've selected Concord Gray Thermal—after working with Steve—for the deceased wife.

The newly married pair had had to stay in Montpelier overnight, as if on the sly, to buy her headstone.

"It still hurts," the wife says, when they're back on the road. "I wonder what's wrong."

Gently, from time to time, the husband had placed firm pressure to a point slightly below the tilt of the new wife's torso at the pubic bone.

At Greg's Place en route to Westport where they live, the wife says, "This wine is sour if you'd like to taste it." She says, "Maybe the doctor injured my tooth."

41

Akin to their lion mask front door pull, they both have brown circles under their eyes and yellowed teeth.

Indignation shows on the lower ledge of the wife's eyes. Her pointed chin is so unlike her predecessor's.

"What are you doing?" the husband says.

"I am checking out my jawbone."

Her husband turned his head this way, away from her, half-pleased. Then the thought came to him. He still hesitated. He did not want to rush. He wanted to live a little.

RELIGIOUS BEHAVIOR

"You think you are a do-gooder," Mother said, "don't you? You're a do-gooder."

After a minute, no more, a newcomer looked toward me, a toddler with *her* mother, I'd bet.

"These type of people," Mother said.

"See that large bird?" I said.

"I don't know," Mother said.

The toddler acted as if she knew me.

It's so interesting when a little person is so clearly distinguished. I can tell—by the superciliary arches above her eyes, the ultra-tiny hands. I regard this visitant as unreal.

HIGHLIGHTS OF THE TWILIGHT

The clerk reminded me of my dead husband who used to say he was always going around all the time with his penis sticking out and that he didn't know what to do.

"Lady!" the clerk said.

A little old lady jerked herself toward that clerk.

A motley group of us was looking at a wristwatch and inwardly I prayed I'd see a glow of dancing matter to lead me. I am another little old lady.

"Mrs. Cook," a clerk said, "are you here to have some fun?"

This is a shop with a bird on a branch in diamonds and pearls, a ruby-eyed dog, a ram's head, a griffin, a cupid in gold.

"It'll be entirely discounted if I understand you correctly—" my clerk said, "this is all that you want!"

"I can't afford it and I'll have that one!"

"You've broken it! You've ruined it!" the clerk said.

I said, "Don't look so awful," but he had already so imprudently advanced into my hell-hole.

THE NEWLY MADE SUPPER

The guest's only wish is to see anyone who looks like Betsy, to put his hands around this Betsy's waist, on her breasts. He's just lost a Betsy. He followed Betsy.

In front of Betsy, who supports on her knees her dinner dish, you can see the guest approach.

"You got your supper?" he says, "Betsy?"

And Betsy says, "Who's that in the purple shirt?"

"That's not purple. You say purple?" says the guest.

"What color would you say that is?" says Betsy.

"That's magenta."

"I have to look that up. Magenta!" says Betsy.

"That's magenta," says the guest.

"That's lavender," says another woman who's a better Betsy.

PONYTAIL

The woman secured her hairs together in a string. The child ate a donut. The woman suggested someone throw a ball. The woman fetched the ball, and then the woman fetched the child, and she bunched up a section of the child's T-shirt, as she bunched up a section of the child's neck, and she secured the child.

CHICKEN WINCHELL

The waitress who is badly nourished or just naturally unhealthy has a theory about why the daughter never returned.

The daughter did return, for only a little stay, to ask which chicken dish her father had ordered for her.

The mother experiences her losses with positivity. She even frames the notion of her own charm as she heads into her normal amount of it.

Yes, she confides in the waitress, both her daughter and her husband have disappeared, and yes, her daughter is a darling, but hasn't she made it clear to her there isn't a boy her age to admire her within a hundred miles?

The mother roams home, wearing the fine check jacket and her black calf heels, alone.

She sees the pair of doors of a little shop where they are selling magic and all kinds of things. Inside, the clerks with elf-locks are dressed for the cold. There is a bakery the mother thinks would be nice and warm. It is okay, and after that, she goes to the gift shop, and gets those sole inserts.

Normally, the family's frugal. They eat at home, buy groceries.

The mother's legs are trembling, yet she has a good conscience and a long life.

She used to weigh one hundred and thirty-five pounds. Now she weighs one hundred and fourteen pounds, but it's been very hectic.

As she sleeps, the telephone rings, wakes her, and she thirsts for a glass of water. She finds that one thing neatly, reasonably, takes her away from yet another.

THE EMPORIUM

I had stretched my body into a dart, inhaled deeply, and passed through the aisles at top speed and then a man with a red-nailed woman and a girl came up to me, and the man said, "You don't remember me! I'm Kevin! I was married to Cynthia. We're not together any more."

They had been the Crossticks!

What he wanted now, Kevin said, was peace, prosperity, and freedom.

And I more or less respected Cynthia Crosstick. I didn't like her at first. She is not very nice. She's odd, but that's the whole point.

I didn't like my fly brooch at first either. It's fake. You can't get it wet. It's very rare and the colors are not nice and I get lots of enjoyment from that.

I picked up Glad Steaming Bags and Rocket Cheese.

"It's very cold. Do you want some lemonade?—" said a child at a little stand, "we give twenty percent to charity."

"No!" I said loudly, as I exited the emporium, although there might have been something to enjoy in swallowing that color.

"Why is she crying?" the child had asked an adult.

Why was I crying?

I had tried to hear the answer, but could not have heard the answer, without squatting—without my getting around down in front of the pair, bending at the knee, so that the proverbial snake no longer crawls on its belly.

I should have first stooped over.

The lemonade girl hadn't mentioned the gumdrop cookies they had hoisted for sale.

Just the mention of cookies brings back memories of Spritz and Springerle and Cinnamon Stars—party favors—attractive, deliciously rich, beautiful colors, very well liked, extra special that I made a struggle to run from.

GIVE THEM STUFF

I ate everything I had and had cramps that somehow fitted together. PIE was on the sign. This was well beyond where the poor people live in their hamlet. PIES VEGETABLES. A woman who took orders there popped a lozenge the color of bixbite into her mouth.

She wore a hat, tasseled magnificently.

In the style of a train trip, we take other trips or a car trip or we go away in a fictitious form.

We're not sure how many parts or places can be put past us—but all this I slyly enjoy.

I think of intimate friends from days gone by and how exquisitely my pie has been traveled.

THE DUCK

I am a disappointment, so I drank the milk. I finished the milk quickly, and then took a low dosage of the tea. I lit a lamp—nearly blushed in the company of myself.

With this sort of blow, I am very unpleasant. Delmore and Constantine know how unpleasant I am.

On such a night, I normally display figurines on the table—a bear holding a staff; a man holding a house; a man holding a house standing on another man—you know, how birds sit on each other.

Constantine—one of the finest men I'll ever know—walked in my direction like a duck who's wrung himself out. My recommendation to the duck would have been—don't fly alone and why fly so high. Do the other ducks know you're out here on your own? Do you even know where the other fucks are? Are you looking for the other fucks?

IF YOU EVER GET
THREE OR FOUR LAUGHING
YOU WEREN'T SOON TO FORGET IT

Marg Foo had been flirtatious with me once. Now she sits in her Avenger as if it were an upright chair and tells me, "What could you do so that I would forgive you?"

So, now it's show time. In the best of times we are nibbling. Fix your mind on the sweep of the action—on the swish, on the smash, and the bang.

Marg left, perhaps for the rest of her life.

Tim kept to himself. Gertrude married again.

I am going to pick up Mr. Reed in the basement.

PROTECTION, PREVENTION, GAZING, GRATIFIED DESIRE

Vera Quilt knows the princes she says. There was some big event—a horse with plumes, and soldiers with ruby buttons, shiny helmets, and swords—when she met them.

If there had been any doubt about my feelings for Vera, now there was not. I looked at her warmly.

The air was cold and I mention this because this is a miniature world with levels of experience where people may starve to death.

At some distance from us there was a mob of people—they're wonderful people—and broad-leaved evergreens, and a flock of birds behaving normally.

"Hoo! —hoo!" Vera began again.

"Now, what do you want, Vera?" I said. Vera and I—we resolve everything in under an hour. She said, "I talked to my husband. It is too hard for me. I come home and it's late and I am tired and he is tired."

And, truly, it's as if people put big branches out on the ground so that Vera can practice climbing on them. You should know that her mind bubbles up in her brain, showing movement, lift! It comes about this way—her confidence, all of it that goes to make a woman.

A large vein showing on her hand curves around her knuckle. She had a cuticle nippers in her hand. Her breath smelt of nothing. Her skull was quite large, but her coat and her skirt were short and there was, pinned to her lapel, a generously sized gemstone flower basket that most people are assuming is a gift from the crown.

"I'd rather not go any farther with you," she said. "I am very tired."

"Exactly," I said.

However, Vera and I had resolved everything in order to push on. She's the best living woman. It was six o'clock, end of the day, as we smoothed farther into the unknown, which is sometimes described as a plot of evil—cliffs and or swamps overshadowing one another, hideous plateaus, and phosphorescent glimmers. Vera protected, pocketed her nippers, and there are the conquests of happiness to be considered that must be produced in the future, and in a series.

At the level of the street, we looked through the plate glass of the department store, a department store erected on the foundation of a princely court.

Vera is young and she still has her woman's flow and we take a glance at something to watch out for in Macy's window that has bulk. This is no drop in the bucket. You must have heard of the expression—*the apple of my eye?*—And we know how to cry *–Help!*

VICKY SWANKY WAS A BEAUTY

You'd have thought her burden was worthy of her, although she shouldn't keep trying to prove she has common sense.

She's Vicky Swanky. She addressed an envelope and wrote her name and address on it also. She is my ideal, my old friend.

The letters of her script are medium sized with slim loops. Her ovals are clear. There were nicely turned heads.

She is still going through a divorce and her children were running around there.

"I forgot to take a shower," she said. "Do you want to take one with me?"

Since I didn't want to do it, I said no, because I'd get confused, and this is too important.

To repeat—I met up with Vicky Swanky whom I hadn't seen in years—who said, "Why don't you come over? I've had systemic lupus erythematosus and when you get through that—"

In connection with sex, we lightened up a little then and we dumped some of it off the edge at a minimum. We could be put through a few strokes like everyone else amid the overall circulation of water.

Human bodies are just not good enough!—and in this way we represented two weak powers.

She has adult-sized fist-sized hands with smooth joints. She has smaller than normal hands. Her hands are not smaller than my hands.

I brought Lee over in the late afternoon, the dog. He has the disposition to avoid conflict, is good-natured, and sets a fine example.

It was getting busy concerning the basic meaning, the degree, and the quality. And by late afternoon, the snow was staying on the surface. No one knows that any better.

Cruelly, I've seen nothing in the book I am reading—about me. I need to see specifically my life with pointers in the book.

May I suddenly drop in on Vicky Swanky and ask for favors?

Years ago Vicky Swanky was a beauty.

Now, here, there were vases of blanket flowers, pancakes. I am so confused here.

She served us pancakes and syrup and coffee and milk and butter. Her breasts were flat. Her hips were flat. She looked older than her forty years and she plays with all of us.

She has a strange way of showing it. There was a skirmish. The plumber arrived and he said he'd have to remove everything from the nipple in the wall to the toilet. Vicky Swanky said, "Is it true? One would think perhaps you might. I thought so. You were right to tell me. I won't enjoy it very much. Naturally enough I can find that out for myself," she said.

CARNEGIE NAIL

Doubtless, early on, in the ultra-fine beginning of the day, others were spectators as I withdrew into Carnegie Nail and I showed the coarseness of my nature in a new sense, for I kept my hands forever forward until at Mrs. Oh's behest, Dee took them.

As a courtesy, to some extent, Mrs. Oh kept her cell phone conversation brief and her voice low.

Mr. Oh sat unspeaking in an aimless, I mean, armless chair. He was less husky than I would have expected—composed, nonetheless, of curving segments. Then, as if by the flip of a lever, he fell from his chair.

Others jumped around.

Strangest of all, whoever enters Carnegie Nail is exempted from the bitterness of experience.

Oh, Mr. Oh found his way back up to good effect while Mimi supported the shop's potted, toppled plant.

The damp day got me as I left, but I did not publicly condemn it.

At home Wanda appeared with our infant and the infant's father—my husband—was seated in a chair that's sufficient to defend itself.

My next step surely was clear, for life presents the flowers of life. We'd been viewing the infant as if it'd been wrenched off a tree branch or a weedy stem.

But the question is much more complex. A child needs to be cut down to its lowest point compatible with survival.

STOP WHEN THE PERSON
BECOMES RESTLESS OR IRRITABLE

I have this violent reaction to Margot Alphonse.

"Perhaps you'll get treated," she had said, "and then you won't have blood all over your hands."

In any event, Margot cancelled her appearance in this story. She had loved me, possibly… bathed me in the bathroom. We slept with a window open—on a pretty courtyard—where you can still hear the people who often need to significantly yell on the avenue.

On the improvement of my understanding of her and over-all, I feel the variety of emotions.

Her voice is heavy. I had intended to lift it, to hold it, so it wouldn't feel as if it was pulling at my neck.

My ethical standards are high.

"What shall we do now?" Margot asked. "I am returning your property."

"No. No, you don't, Margot."

She opened up her handbag and handed me my stonewalls, it felt like.

STAND

My friend said, "I fell in love with the neighbor."

I said, "Your husband fell in love with the neighbor?"

My friend said, "No!" She said, "*I* fell in love with the neighbor!"

She was counting her fingers. She said she couldn't get the neighbor's penis to do anything.

As a matter of fact, I couldn't get his penis to do anything either. It hung like a mop or it had a life of its own. How it came up in the first place, I don't know. He couldn't get my vagina—I wanted to say—to utter a word.

But since one should always make room for fun, we all ate food and we laughed.

The last time I saw my friend was when she was finishing her drink, gulping. Was it like the sound of the sea perhaps?—how the sea very slowly and with great effort laps but does not go down—I want to say—in one gulp.

The last time I saw my friend's crêpe de chine skin, her frizzy hair—her dark breasts that wriggle raw, I said to myself, "You had enough?"

ONE OF THE GREAT DRAWBACKS

He had just seen a rodent with such expressive eyes and he knows horses intimately, too. He carves horses and he paints a whole group on their points of hips, the throatlatches, on the tails, and so forth.

His daughter and his daughter's friend have stopped by briefly.

If left to themselves, they fight like fiends or yell out the great news and one of these girls is entirely out of danger.

The daughter hates her father and she says, "Dad, sorry, but you should keep trying me—"

He knows a horse seems to be laboring when its legs are drawn up under it—he knows that.

His daughter has a terrified pair of eyes.

A Delta Airlines employee arrives to deliver his lost piece of luggage.

The father blushes—congratulates himself for getting so much attention, is so stimulated, and ever since has felt irremediably shy when sexual subjects are discussed.

COMMON BODY

So, I've got good news, but I also felt so bad I was crying.

She's so wrongly old and I'm her daughter, but can she still have children?

HUMAN BEING

Now I have a baby boy and a five-year-old girl.

Being married, I thought I'd always be married to Wayne because he tried to be perfect. What more could he ask for?

I LIKE THE FRINGE

They don't need to get me more belts. I have enough belts. I like the fringe.

This is to commemorate personal tastes—mine—the Durrants'. The Durrants are still here.

Mrs. Durrant asks Gabor Mavor what she wants and Gabor says, "A watch."

I wish I had Gabor's health and safety.

However, I am encouraged by the spirit of invention. A man I see through the plate glass shovels a lot of snow and he doesn't even have a shovel! He has one of those little brush scrapers on a stick.

A man like this has self-confidence.

Often life deals severely with me, and yet I'll be wearing my nose.

RUDE

There's a cloth to wipe clear her muscular organ with the foam or the scum on it. People were talking too loudly. "You can't tell grown up people what to do," someone said. One person had fever, pain in the abdomen that develops normally like a sixth sense, and he wasn't careful choosing a marriage partner. He is noted for his humor and his favorite color is dark purple.

The physician covering him called him to report: "I find myself shocked and deeply hurt by your condition."

MRS. KEABLE'S BROTHERS

Her fate was being rigged for the rough surface. Nothing was omitted from her desirable world insofar as she likes Mr. Keable and other men in suits with short hair; patient service staff who smile; all the people with large, accurate vocabularies; big blossoms; logical arguments.

If a poached egg, open and bleeding, could give us the color palette, let us color her home in with that.

In the evening, Mrs. Keable's brothers, arriving in a black Volkswagen, often visited. She had in the past been scared to death of them.

As the sun comes up, it's as if, for Mrs. Keable, there's a slice of lime on any serving of her food.

NEW LIFE FROM DEAD THINGS

See how the kitchen spray looks when it's turned into words?—white or buff and gray.

The daughter leant over a hope chest to confirm the location of the electrical outlet.

It doesn't make my life worse to say that the mother seems to enjoy herself and that the daughter is fine. The previous autumn there'd been difficulties. The daughter fled and did not plan to return. The grave of the woman's husband had been recently dug.

The daughter's dead now.

The mother poured herself a cup of coffee and studied the meniscus and I sized it up, too.

I tried to see how I could run off into my own words.

Don't hurt me!

NONE OF THIS WOULD HAVE BEEN
REMOTELY FEASIBLE

I'm smart, I think, and I am always up for fun and games—
jokes. So this is suitable for certain people. One day the police
found me in a pile of snow and I said I don't want to live any-
more. Mother gave me a hot drink, a bath, washed my clothes,
and ironed them. We had a long talk—she saved my life. I was
going to find another snowdrift.

This morning I walked toward a tree. A woman at a distance was standing in the snow, crying, "Melba! Melba!"
That's what I thought.

"Do you want me to get her for you?" I called. I called
again and I called again to the woman just to make sure.

"What would I have done?" she said. "I would have had to
go way over there and around, but I just can't!"

"Don't let go of her leash!" I said, and turned away.

After a pause, I looked into the world, but I never found them.

TAN BAG

The Almighty doesn't spoil everything—for I saw sky-high things—a tan bag, paper. I woke up dizzy. Mrs. Billyboy said the room was going around. Took her to the doctor. She got examined and is OK now.

It is my business to comfort the lady.

Chasteness, more pampering, I must get married. I changed her sheets.

But this is not a lamentation. In this way, her story is handed on to you.

She had a good day; had dental done. Dinner is chicken winglets, pea loaf, and Peppermint Pattie.

Spring is. Summer is.

Madam used hibiscus, as a girl, to make her lips red, the soot of the candlewick to shadow her eyes, candle wax for her brows.

Her winter coat waves all its arms at us! Her camel duffle makes the sound of matchsticks being struck—if that helps.

ARM UNDER THE SOIL

It might seem to me that Chuck and I have a very happy marriage, which I cannot, I cannot believe I believe that.

I had gone out to look at what Chuck calls the dot plants—things out of proportion with the ground for which they are intended.

They're a focal feature to form the centerpiece among the many plants that are not valued. In the house, he has his cascade bonsai tree on a high stand.

I could not get between him and what he was in front of and I found myself waiting on some joyous occasion.

By the close of the day, I had no idea how to be practical. I'd lost control of my life.

Chuck tapped me, saying, "Who is that woman? What did she want?"

It had been our neighbor. I wish she had been thinking highly of me, while her husband looked on, forlorn in the car. "Your quack grass!" she had cried. "Why don't you just let me kill it for you?"

They have a rock garden, steppingstones, a perennial border, and then I could see that our weeds were menacing those.

The suspense in that moment had drawn me in and I was fascinated to hear my answer to her that was delivered in a weepy form.

In addition to the quack grass, we also have plantain, chickweed, thyme-leaved speedwell—curiously green and brown.

I understand. Hunks and slabs of weeds are not enjoyable to view.

Pressing the heel of my hand against my trowel, with a quick motion of the wrist and forearm, I repeat the motion. I am jabbing side to side. The tissues attached to the stem are softened enough for the root to be slipped out, so that I may remove my muscle section.

BEING STARED AT

I was ready during the reunion back at his house in April and I had a feeling he was present.

Most curiously he had asked us to call him Uncle Chew and I'd been fond of him.

The elderberry lemonade reminded me of when we were young inductees to the religious world and we sat around here. I was very impressed by the box lunch.

They handed out sheets with the lyrics to the song we'd written as a farewell for Uncle Chew. A part was missing.

When we arrived at this reunion it was chilly. The next day warmer. The next day chilly. The day after, I had a speech to make. We had hiked a certain distance past the church doorway, the hearth, the courtyard, along the village lane, the rough brick wall. I saw the same backdrop more than once so that I got my bearings. I was a woman in a fur collar and false hair, reminiscing.

They handed out lunch-box sandwiches as I came slowly down the length of my time, which I have become very attached to, and my memories and my remarks—hurt my pride.

EXPECTANT MOTHERHOOD

I don't like them or my brother. My children don't like me.

I count the affronts, mindful not to give up all my views. I'd rather contort my guts. Conditions are somewhat unfavorable, despite strengths. I'd feel so much better if Brucie influenced me.

There is a side to me they have not been exposed to. I mention this. They take up their tasks. In short, my daughter told me to wait a minute, that she'd join me.

I said, "No!"

She put her head back and closed her coat at the neck. "I wonder if you realize..." she said. It took me a moment to.

Everyone else was hurrying. We stood. She was leaning against the mantelpiece. "Why are you so unpleasant?"

I answered, "I don't wish you well."

I threw my gloves on the floor and my hat. I had been wearing my dark blue coat. Drops of moisture were on our windows, and fog. We are a family. There's a point to it and to the dimmer switch in the foyer. The next thing—my daughter was stepping along the corridor and out the door. I seriously did not think I was in the state I describe as reserved for me.

COMFORT

She made assurances that satisfied her ambitions—saw the body interred, spent the rest of the week asking questions, suggesting action. She visited with her family and reminisced.

Getting routine matters out of the way, she headed home after buying a grounding plug and ankle wrist weights.

She fed the dog and put the boys to bed. Allen didn't go to work.

She received a call from a woman whose sister had died.

She made some of those unequaled assurances, was escorted with the family to the grave. People seem to respond to her. She talked with them, gave a woman a played-out peck on the cheek.

Getting routine matters out of the way, she attained riches, social position, power, studied for an hour or so, cleaned up, took the family to a movie, after which she forecasted her own death with a lively narration that gave her gooseflesh.

She felt raw, pink and so fresh!

THE STRENGTH

"I am going to cough," I said. "Cough, cough."

I left Mary, my mother, to experience that by herself and went to get the dish—a lion couchant—with a slew of nuts in it, and I served us wine, and I coughed.

Mary put her hand on the top of her head, as if she could not rightly rest it there.

"Mary, how are you, Mary?" I said. "Now, Mary."

"Not so good," she replied. "I've just been lying around."

Then she changed into the shape she pleased—an upright, independent person.

My father, her husband—we were surprised—walked in, buttoning himself to depart. I had thought he was dead. His bad foot had killed him.

My mother and my dead father provide strength for me. They recklessly challenge their competency.

It is senseless to prevent them.

THIS HAS TO BE THE BEST

It isn't until a Bengal cat comes by—the Sheepshanks' cat Andy—that I can see my way in the dark so to speak.

This flame design decorates almost all of his body and the brilliancy demonstrates exceptional technique.

When I pet the cat, I rough up too much of the detail, and the cat is yelling at me.

I went to the sex shop after. I know the saleswoman there very well.

And yet Brenda said, "I have never seen you before in my whole life!"

This must be on account of the harsh light.

A MAN, AN ANIMAL

At the cinema I watched closely the camels, the horses, the young actor taking his stance for the sexual act.

He started up with a pretty girl we had a general view of.

I felt the girl's pallor stick into me.

Another girl, in pink swirls alternating with yellow swirls, intruded.

The girls were like the women who will one day have to have round-the-clock duty at weddings, at birthdays, at days for the feasts.

Unaccountably, I hesitated on the last step of the cinema's escalator when we were on our way out, and several persons bumped into me.

An ugly day today—I didn't mention that, with fifty mile per hour winds.

But here is one of the more fortunate facts: We were Mr. and Mrs. Gray heading home.

It has been said—the doors of a house should always swing into a room. They should open easily to give the impression to those entering that everything experienced inside will be just as easy.

A servant girl was whipping something up when we arrived, and she carried around the bowl with her head bowed.

We've been told not to grab at breasts.

Before leaving for Indiana in the morning—where I had to clean up arrangements for a convention—I stood near my wife to hear her speak. So, who is she and what can I expect further from her?

What she did, what she said in the next days, weeks and years, addresses the questions Americans are insistently, even obsessively asking—but what sorts of pains in the neck have I got?

Please forgive our confusion and our failures. We make our petitions—say our prayers. It's like our falling against a wall, in a sense.

On a recent day, my wife gave me a new scarf to wear as a present. It's chrome green. Her mother Della, on that same day, had helped her to adjust to her hatred of me.

I'd have to say, I've given my wife a few very pleasant shocks, too.

SHELTER

Derek is somebody everybody loves because everybody loves what Derek loves and he is handsome. I've left Derek behind on the veranda, in the vestibule, in the passage. He is fifty-two years old and behaving properly. Every day he thinks of what to do and wonderfully he tries to do it. I can make out his force, his shape. He sits at a shrewd distance from the dining parlor, now.

I poured myself a cup of coffee (none for Derek), bad tasting, that satisfies my hunger.

Oh fine—pretty rooms, opening out on either side. I am refreshed, filled with sweet feelings, enjoying a revival, long and looping, and I pull a door shut and take slower steps, as if walking to my bus stop.

I'll be unmanageable at the back stair's spiral.

Not a correct use of this residence.

But how odd it is—I recorked a bottle and stowed a jar of mayonnaise and Derek came in here for a particular reason.

Derek's task is to provide continuity room to room—thoughtfully—consistent with ensuring that no violent breaks occur and shouldn't I appreciate this?

Also, the recent calming wave of walls and ceilings has helped me very much.

However, the shovel and tongs, upright against the mantelpiece, you could argue that they just don't belong!

I make every effort not to crack or to split and to fit in, albeit, fitfully.

ENORMOUSLY PLEASED

Like this—leaning forward—she spit into a tulip bed within a block of Capital One—with her head like this.

Passing Rudi's, she saw the barbers in their barber chairs—four, five of them—in royal blue smocks—they had fallen asleep.

There are so many more things like that. She had spent the morning with the problem of sex.

Now she was making her progress into town. The sun was low. In any case, the weather—there are so many more things like that.

The woman made her progress as if she were an ordinary woman who was not aware of all her good fortune. The pear trees in bloom looked to her like clusters or fluff. She saw more things like that, that were complete successes.

She had spit into the tulip bed, as so often happens in life, with verve, and that was fun. Neither was the sun too low or too cold.

The documents she signed at Capital One glittered like certain leaves, like some flowers. That bending, that signing had hurt her back. She had more money as of today in her everyday life and she was tucking her hair and bending her hair as she had so often planned.

When she awakened that morning, she had smoothed her hair—when semi-alert—but she was still capable of adventures and their central thrust and with some encouragement, the penis of her husband had been leaning its head forward and plucking at her.

The barbers in their smocks, in the town, had awakened and were busy with their customers. And, she's a doctor!—or a lawyer!—with only a few griefs to her name. She's great!

If we trace the early years of her life, the intricacies, the dark years, the large middle zone, the wide-spacing between the fluctuations, as between her progress and her verve—the balanced tension—we see that the woman turns everyday life into daydreams, trusts in the future, is gullible and has some emotional immaturity.

HELLO! HI! HELLO!

My association with Moffat was the luxury of my life or a decorative keynote—a postage stamp.

On Moffat's recommendation I took a meal alone at Cheiro's Café. I drank ginger ale with my black cherry linzer. I ate one fried egg and that felt as if I was eating a postage stamp—with its flat ridges.

I had begged Moffat, to be completely fair, to keep on with having what he called fun with me. Although, I have a respectful attitude toward the public status of the person addressed, he had become, he said, disentranced.

There is a reasonable code of conduct concerning Moffat.

I found I was a bit cold-pigged—drained, not dried entirely.

I came to rest in front of the elegant Blue Tree.

I had on a gather skirt—steeped in red—a blouse with a series of buttons, hair combed. I noted my showy, stylish approach in the shop window glass with relieved surprise.

Once inside, I bought a simulated coral and onyx necklace, colorless beads, another necklace with swiftly flowing floral decorations, with ruby and gold glints that gives me a liberally watered shine.

When exiting, I studied trifling clouds stacked deliberately.

By and by, Moffat came along, popping out his fingers bouquet-style and calling my name.

He made a simultaneous outward swipe, with both his hands, with his fingers spread.

What a darling! No bad side. He has a strong activity level and a good sense of presentation and he's tentatively changed his mind—about me!

He's added, throughout his life, quite a rare group of us to his collection.

Penelope, for one, has a coiffure with a small, japanned bun and she's very neatly sweet.

My intention, with my own flourishes, is to create an impression of frankness and ambition.

I am prepared to be examined again.

I should be observed strongly and for a long time, so they can see the changes of my colors during the goings-on.

DEFEAT

One Healdsburg Taxicab arrived while she put three wide, wide pieces of paper into her waste can. A peculiarly restricted number of flowers had been cast into the vase and Julius Minx is now here and he exceeds our space.

AS THE WORLD TURNED OUT

There's usually a side table in the story—a place to put a vase of flowers—or a potted plant—a clock, a book. A late-blooming flower may show up in the story—a swimming pool, a carefully groomed garden, pheasants touring the grounds (I mean peasants), Bella Donnelly, the Fraser family, one-on-one meetings with people enthusiastic about work, laughter and companionship, the great tragedy inflicted when people go under, the notion that even a woman can thrust herself forward and up and so-to-speak out from under on the first step down.

LORD OF THE FACE

The fact that she's backlit makes her look ambitious and she tickles my funny bone.

First I thought that her blue eyes on a pink and yellow background looked a bit purblind, but then their general dimension intrigued me. They have a nice design—glare—and they're not generous.

It's hard to slot him in. He seemed novicelike, uncertain of himself, but he was efficient.

She said, "I am Diane Williams."

They went out to the terrace for a cigarette.

Italy itself is very lovely, but as the brightness of the sun hit the terrace, the figure of a six-legged star—a sign for sure—was produced on the bluestone.

All six legs of the star were fairly straight. One leg of the star was not exactly the same length as the others. One leg was perfectly straight.

Their housekeeper grabbed at her own leg and at the top side of her foot.

Their cat was yanked up off of the terrace by a bird of prey and then dropped!

For the cat's recovery there were five thousand dollars worth of veterinarian bills and for the housekeeper—a premonition she'd be hit by a car.

The star! The cross! The square!

A single sign shows the tendency. Can people avoid disaster? Yes. I leave my readers to draw their own conclusions.

Some years ago, I was satisfied.

Stop!

Diane! So many things are clear. Diane was blushing. Her yellow fuzz shows in the sun. She no longer has words of her own and so chooses grunting. Diane! Open! Contribute! Inform! The place!—her brown fuzz, a yellow fuzz over it. The curtains are original. A room contains medical equipment. Diane's an early type who before arriving in Siena had a day planned for her departure. She had made the arrangements so she'd stay during the spring in Italy as an imaginary character with hope.

The following stories have appeared in *Harper's*: "If You Ever Get Three or Four Laughing You Weren't Soon to Forget It," "As the World Turned Out," "If Told Correctly It Will Center on Me," "Woman in Rose Dress," "Stand," "One of the Great Drawbacks," "My First Real Home" (reprinted from *Post Road*), "Protection, Prevention, Gazing, Gratified Desire," "Human Being," "I Like the Fringe," "Broom," "Rude," "New Life from Dead Things," "Mrs. Keable's Brothers," "None of This Would Have Been Remotely Feasible," "Pedestal," "Between Midnight and 6 AM," "This Has to Be the Best," "Lord of the Face," "Being Stared At," "Give Them Stuff," "Expectant Motherhood," "Glee," "Chicken Winchell."

These stories first appeared, sometimes in a slightly different form or with a different title, in: *Agriculture Reader*: "Highlights of the Twilight"; *The Brooklyn Rail*: "Cockeyed" (originally "She Could Never Have Found a Better or More Delightful One"); *Conjunctions*: "Ponytail" (originally "Virtue"), "The Newly Made Supper," "The Use of Fetishes," "Stop When the Person Becomes Restless or Irritable," "Weight, Hair, Length"; *Esquire* online: "The Duck"; *Gigantic*: "Mood Which Gripped Me"; *The Lifted Brow*: "Defeat," "Common Body"; *McSweeney's*: "A Man, An Animal," "Arm Under the Soil," "Death Bed" (originally "For Now I Was Tall"), "Enormously Pleased," "Hello! Hi! Hello!," "My Defects," "Shelter," "The Strength," "Tan Bag," "Vicky Swanky Was a Beauty"; *Post Road*: "My First Real Home"; *Rampike*: "Comfort," "The Emporium," "On the Job"; *Sleepingfish*: "Carnegie Nail"; *Triple Canopy*: "Religious Behavior"; *Western Humanities Review*: "The Wedding Mask Door Pull."

"My First Real Home," was also reprinted in *The Pushcart Prize XXXIV: Best of the Small Presses*, 2010.

ABOUT THE AUTHOR

Diane Williams is the author of six previous books, and the publisher and founding editor of the literary annual *NOON*. She has taught at Bard College, Syracuse University, and the Center for Fiction. She lives in New York City.